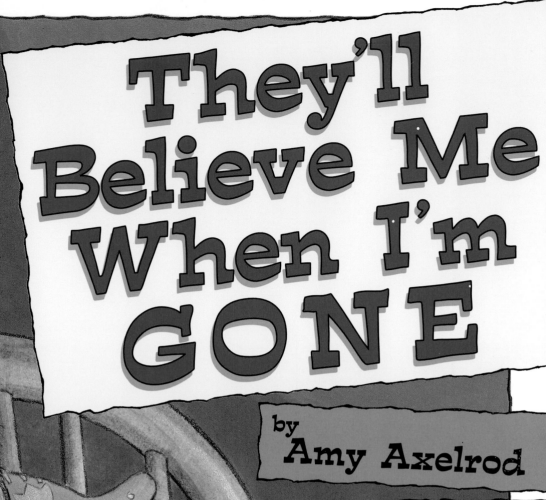

They'll Believe Me When I'm GONE

by Amy Axelrod

illustrated by Jack E. Davis

GALACTIC TRAVEL MADE EASY!

OUTER SPACE VACATION SPOTS

DUTTON CHILDREN'S BOOKS
New York

Text copyright © 2003 by Amy Axelrod
Illustrations copyright © 2003 by Jack E. Davis

CIP Data is available.

Published in the United States 2003 by Dutton Children's Books,
a division of Penguin Putnam Books for Young Readers
345 Hudson Street, New York, New York 10014
www.penguinputnam.com
Typography by Richard Amari

Manufactured in Hong Kong
First Edition
1 3 5 7 9 10 8 6 4 2
ISBN 0-525-46660-6

For Pumpkin
A. A.

For Dave and Brenda
J. E. D.

They'll miss me when I'm gone.

"My ride is coming tonight," I announce at breakfast.

"Sure," says my brother, Gordon. "The only ride that's coming for you is the school bus."

"Flying saucers don't send secret signals to little boys, Max," my father reminds me for about the hundredth time.

"Should I pack a bag for you while you're at school?" my mother jokes. "Just in case?"

"Actually, that's a very good idea," I tell her.

They can laugh all they want. Who needs them? Soon I'll have a new family. My new mom won't sniff my face every night to check that I've really washed with soap. She won't even have a nose.

My new dad and I will read each other's minds. He won't need to ask me dumb questions like "So what did you learn in school today?"

Best of all, I won't have to put up with my jerky brother making that scary skeleton face. My new brother's mouth will be very tiny.

None of the kids in my class believe me, even though I'm an expert about space.

My teacher thinks I daydream too much. Then how did I win first prize in the science fair?

At least my best friend, Herbie, understands. He wants to be just like me, so we formed a secret club. I taught him everything I know about aliens. We practice signaling to them when it's dark.

Gordon and his friends are so stupid. "Say hello to the little green men for us," they say, laughing.

Everyone knows aliens aren't green.

"Can I have your basketball when you go?" my brother asks.

"No way. I'll be needing it."

"This is the last time I'll ever eat broccoli," I say at dinner. "Don't you want to grow up nice and tall?" my dad asks. "Who cares? I'm already the same height as my new family."

"What do you think the aliens are gonna do," Gordon says with a snort, "let you eat candy and ice cream all day long?"

"Dunno," I say, "but I wouldn't laugh if I were you. Because when I'm gone, Mom'll be looking for someone to eat my vegetables."

"I guess I won't be tucking you in anymore," my mother says, sniffing my face.

"Yup," I answer.

"Will your new mom read stories with you like I do?"

"Thanks for reminding me to pack some books," I say.

"And will she snuggle up close and give you a million kisses, one for each star in the sky?"

"Mom, there are more than a million stars," I remind her.

"Don't forget to send a post-card!" Gordon screams from his bedroom down the hall. "Oh, and by the way, when you're gone, Mom'll really love me best."

When it's time to go, I wake my parents so I can say good-bye.
I don't bother saying good-bye to my brother.
My mom asks, "Are you wearing clean underwear?"

UNDERWEAR! Like my new family could care less. They don't even wear any.

"Would you like me to go outside and wait with you?" my dad asks.

"Okay," I tell him. "If you want to."

My dad spreads out a blanket so we can lie down and look up at the sky.

"I told you," he says, "there's no spaceship out there. Just lots of bright stars. Look, there's the Big Dipper. It's part of the constellation Ursa Major, which is also called the Great Bear. Did you know that?"

"Yes, Pop. I taught *you* that."

"If a spaceship really did land, are you sure you'd want to leave us?" my dad asks.

"Didn't you ever want to have a really big adventure?" I ask him.

"Once. When I was your age, I wanted to dig a hole all the way to China."

"What was it like there?"

"I never dug the hole. My dad said it was impossible. Hey, what's that constellation over there?"

"That's Orion," I tell him.

"Maybe it's time I got you a new telescope for your..."

Z·Z·Z·Z·Z·Z·Z·Z·